W9-AKE-051

To Nicole Mandrell Shipley,
an answer to a mother's prayers.
And to Clint and Rance Collins,
the godchildren who have
blessed my life beyond compare.
LOUISE

For my sons, Clint and Rance,
who have taught me that
a parent's smiles and tears
are the most precious
of all of God's gifts.
ACE

To all the children
who will touch this book,
may your childhood
be filled with love.
LOUISE AND ACE

All In A Day's Work

All In A Day's

Louise Mandrell and Ace Collins

Children's Holiday Adventure Series
Volume 7

THE SUMMIT GROUP
1227 West Magnolia, Suite 500, Fort Worth, Texas 76104
© 1993 by Louise Mandrell and Ace Collins. All rights reserved.
Printed in the United States of America.

93   10   9   8   7   6   5   4   3   2   1

Jacket and Book Design by Cheryl Corbitt

LIBRARY OF CONGRESS CATALOGING-IN-PUBLICATION DATA
Mandrell, Louise.
    All in a day's work / Louise Mandrell and Ace Collins; illustrated by Don Morris.
    p. cm. – (Louise Mandrell & Ace Collins holiday adventure series; v. 7)
    Summary: Rance and Kelly don't appreciate everything their mother does for them, until their
scramble to find her a special gift for Mother's Day opens their eyes to her importance.
    ISBN 1-56530-036-X: $12.95
    [1. Mother and child – Fiction. 2. Mother's Day – Fiction.] I. Collins, Ace. II. Morris, Don,
ill. III. Title. IV. Series: Mandrell, Louise. Louise Mandrell & Ace Collins holiday adventure
series; v. 7.
PZ7. M31254Al   1993
[Fic] – dc20   93-310
CIP
AC

Work

Illustrated by Don Morris

THE SUMMIT GROUP ⌐

Rance McGill sat squirming in his seat. It was Friday, almost 3:15, time for school to let out for another week. How he hated the last ten minutes of class! How he wanted to get out in the May afternoon sun! Though his eyes were on Mrs. Divin, his thoughts were on baseball. The first game of the little league season was next week, and he was going to be the starting pitcher.

"Rance," a distant voice called.

The blonde-haired boy didn't hear. He was dreaming of being at the plate in the last inning with the bases loaded and his team behind by three runs.

"Rance McGill!" Mrs. Divin said more sharply, waking the boy up to the reality of the moment. "Would you please come to the front of the room?"

Slowly Rance got up from his seat and walked to where his teacher stood. He didn't know what he had done, but he figured that he must be in trouble. Why else would Mrs. Divin call him up to her desk? As he stood there in front of his classmates, he waited for his teacher to begin scolding. As the seconds dragged by, he wondered, "What did I forget to do?"

"As you know, class," Mrs. Divin explained, "we recently sold flower seeds to raise money for new playground equipment. The swings and the slide will be here next week." As the class clapped and cheered, Mrs. Divin smiled and held up her hand to quiet their enthusiasm. "And Rance sold more packets of seeds than anyone in school. That makes him the winner of our grand prize, a new ball glove!"

Pulling the brand new, golden leather mitt out of her desk, she held it up in the air and announced, "This is not just any ball glove. You can't buy *this* one in a store. It was donated to the school by the record-setting pitcher of the Texas Rangers, Nolan Ryan. It's a glove he has worn in a game, and he autographed it right here on the top. For those of you who don't follow baseball, Nolan Ryan has more strike-outs than any other major league player ever."

With a puzzled look on her face, Suzy Dunn held up her hand. Mrs. Divin pointed to the girl and asked, "What is it?"

"Why," Suzy questioned, "would anyone want a glove from someone who strikes out all the time? Doesn't that mean he's not very good?"

The room broke out in laughter. Smiling, Mrs. Divin explained, "Nolan Ryan is a pitcher. His *job* is to strike people out."

All this was lost on Rance. He was too busy admiring the glove. He couldn't wait to show it to his sister and his dad. He cared little that he hadn't sold very many seeds. Actually, his mother had done the selling. She had taken them to work, to church, and to her club meetings. She had asked everyone she knew to buy them. But Rance wasn't thinking about that. He was thrilled to have the grand prize. The glove was his, and so was the reputation that went with it. Now he would really be a great ball player!

"Rance," the teacher smiled, "thank you for all your hard work. Now you may take your seat. Children, don't forget to take home the paper weights we made in art this week. They are for your mothers on Mother's Day."

As Rance returned to his seat his thoughts were not on anything but his new glove. Never had he had such a special prize. He was so caught up in studying every stitch, that he didn't even hear the bell ring. But the other kids did, and they gathered around Rance as if he were Santa Claus. They couldn't wait to see the glove.

After showing it off to every student in school, Rance practically flew home. Once there, he found an old ball and sat on the couch tossing it into his glove.

"Anybody home?" Kelly shouted as she charged in the back door. Usually Rance ignored his twelve-year-old sister, but today was different. He couldn't wait to show her.

"What is it this time, another frog?" Kelly asked.

Shaking his head, Rance answered, "No, it's a genuine Nolan Ryan major league glove, and it has his real autograph."

"Sure," Kelly replied.

"No," Rance argued as he jumped off the couch and ran over to meet her. "I'm serious. Remember those seeds I sold for playground equipment? Well, I got this for selling the most."

"You didn't sell them," his sister laughed. "Mom did. You should give the glove to her."

"She did it for me," a tight-lipped Rance growled, "so it's mine. Besides, what would she do with it?"

"Who cares about an old ball glove anyway," Kelly shrugged. "Have you got any money?"

"No," Rance responded, "and even if I did I wouldn't give it to someone who doesn't like baseball."

"What happened to that money you had in your room?" Kelly asked.

"I spent it on a video game," he answered as he lay back down on the couch and began tossing the ball and catching it again.

"I haven't gotten Mom anything for Mother's Day," she sighed, "and I was hoping that you would make me a loan."

"Sorry," Rance answered. "I made her something at school. It's so cool. You ought to see the way I painted it, I mean . . . ." Then a horrible thought hit him. "I left it at school!" he shouted, jumping to his feet. "Quick! What time is it?"

"4:30."

"The school's already locked up," the boy frowned. But in a moment he shrugged. "No big deal," he announced. "Dad will give me some money. He always makes sure that we have something special for Mom."

"No," Kelly shook her head, "he can't. Don't you remember? He's on a business trip until Monday night. Mom told us that last night at supper."

"I forgot," Rance said. "I sure wish I hadn't left the present at school."

"I sure wish you had some money," his sister replied.

That evening, after Mrs. McGill had gotten home from work and fixed dinner, Rance and his sister met in Kelly's room to talk.

"Where's Mom?" she asked as Rance walked in.

"She's in the basement washing clothes," he answered. Then, looking at the scene around him, he added, "Don't you hang anything up? It looks like a storm hit here. How can you live like this?"

"Oh, really?" Kelly responded sarcastically. "I suppose the fact that your frog stayed lost for two weeks in the mess you call a room means you're a model housekeeper. Your closet is probably classified as a toxic waste dump. Anyway, when our rooms get too bad, Mom will clean them up. She always does. Have you come up with any plans for presents?"

"No," he sighed. Peeking under an old sweater, he asked, "What's this?"

"That's my emergency bank." she answered.

Picking it up, he shook it and exclaimed, "There's money in here!"

"It's for a new outfit to wear to Jenny's party," she answered, seizing the blue piggy bank from his hands.

"We'll use that money," he said. "How much have you got?"

"Twenty dollars," she responded, "but I'm saving it. I earned that money."

"How?" Rance demanded.

"I took care of Mr. Cowden's cat and dog when they were on vacation," she answered.

"No, you didn't," he argued. "You went over once. Mom took care of them the rest of the week. You were either too busy with your friends or too lazy to get out of bed. Let's use that for her present."

"I want a new dress," she challenged.

"What about Mom's present?" Rance insisted.

"Okay, okay," she sighed, "I'll go to the store and find something tomorrow."

"What do you mean *you*?" Rance said. "If you remember, you owe me ten dollars. So a part of this gift is going to be from me."

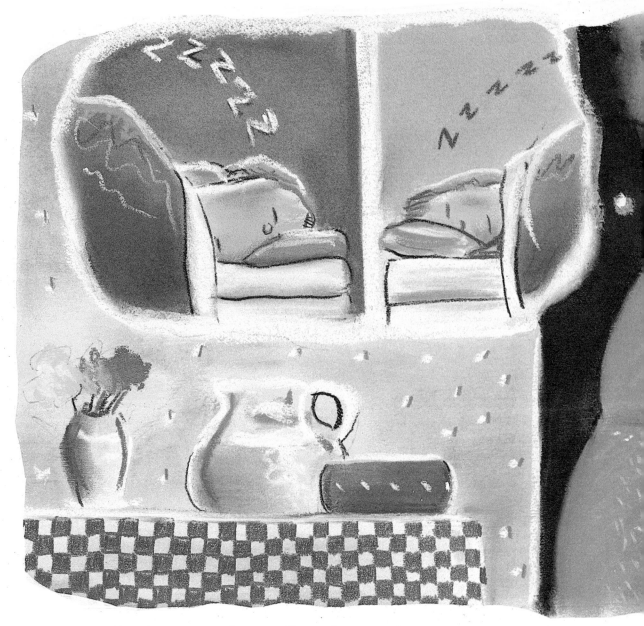

"All right. I remember," Kelly said. "Mom has got to work all day, so why don't we stop by the cleaners and see if we can talk to that lady she works with – Mrs. Roselli. Maybe she will have an idea of what Mom wants. Besides, I've never been down there to see what Mom does."

"It is so easy," Rance informed his sister. "All she does is wait behind that big counter and take people's money when they pick up their clothes."

The next morning Rance and Kelly slept until ten. By the time they got up, their mother had already been at work for three hours. Still, before she had left she had prepared both breakfast and lunch for her kids and left instructions on how to heat them in the microwave oven. Things were just like they always were – Mom thinking of the things her children would need. It was a routine operation that ran so smoothly neither Rance nor Kelly ever noticed this labor of love.

Rance and Kelly started on their way downtown, Rance tossing and catching the ball as they walked.

"I don't know why you had to bring that glove along," Kelly said, watching her brother pitch a ball into the air.

"Because I don't want to lose it," Rance replied. "Besides, it's good practice to walk and catch at the same time."

"I don't know about the practice part," Kelly smiled, "but as many times as you've dropped that ball and had to chase it, it has to be good exercise."

After they had walked for another ten minutes, they came upon a small girl standing all alone at a busy inter- section. They had never seen a child crying as hard as she

was. They watched her for a long time, waiting for someone to join her, but no one did.

"Who do you suppose she is?" Rance asked.

"I don't know," Kelly answered, "but she couldn't be over five or six. We should ask her where she lives."

"Hello," Kelly smiled as she approached the child. "My name is Kelly McGill. Who are you?"

Swallowing a sob, the dark-eyed youngster wiped the tears away and whispered, "I'm Phyllis Watson."

"Are you all alone?" Kelly inquired.

Nodding her head, the girl began to cry again.

"None of that," Kelly grinned. "We'll make everything all right for you. Do you know where you live?"

Nodding her head, Phyllis said, "On Park Street, 115."

"That's on the other side of town," Rance informed his sister. "That's too far to walk."

"I lost Marie," Phyllis sobbed. "She's taking care of me, but I can't find her."

"Was Marie your baby sitter?" Kelly asked.

"Yes," the child answered.

Turning to Rance, Kelly said, "We're going to have to take her home. There's a bus stop about a block up. I can ride with her."

"But that will take a lot of our money," he argued.

"We can't leave her here," she sighed. "You go ahead to the cleaners and try to find something out, and we'll just use the money we have left."

Rance left the two girls at the bus stop and walked another five blocks to the downtown business district. There he found the cleaners where his mother worked. Pushing open the heavy glass door, he waited just inside as his mother handed three suits to an elderly gentleman.

"What a surprise!" She exclaimed, looking over at her son as the man left. "What brings you here?"

"Just wanted to say hi," he replied with a big smile. "Working hard?"

"It has been a busy day," she responded. "I've still got a lot to do, so if you want to visit you'll have to follow me to the back."

Rance followed her behind the counter, through a swinging door, and into a hot room filled with machines and clothes. He watched in amazement as his mother

picked up a heavy basket and dropped its contents into a huge machine. After she started the washer, she laid out a pair of pants on a press.

"It feels like a jungle in here," Rance observed.

"You get used to it," his mother assured him.

Looking around the room, the boy was surprised to see that there were no other people working. "Don't you have anyone to help you?"

"No, on most days I do it by myself," she replied. Hearing a bell, his mother stopped her work and ran to the front of the store. Rance followed her. Another customer had come in to drop off some laundry. After the woman left, Rance, hoping to lighten his mother's load, made an offer.

"Why don't we go to lunch together?"

"I'd love to," Joan replied, "but I can't leave the shop. I've got too much to do."

"You mean you have to lift more of those heavy baskets?" he asked.

"About a hundred more," she laughed.

"And you have to press more pants?" he questioned.

"A lot," she smiled. "It's what I do every day."

Nodding his head, Rance moved toward the door. As he left, his mother smiled and returned to the back room.

An hour later Kelly found Rance in the gift store.

"What kept you?" Rance asked as he tossed his baseball up in the air and caught it in his new glove.

"It was a long way over there," Kelly explained, "and no one was home. I found a neighbor who was a good friend of the family and left Phyllis with her. I gave her our address and phone number just in case her mother didn't return. Anyway, have you found anything for Mom?"

"Nothing that's good enough," he sighed. "Do you know how hard she works?"

"You said that she had an easy job," Kelly answered.

"Never mind what I said," he answered. "I watched her. She works harder than anyone I know. She does a lot more than I thought. Anyway, how much money have you got left?"

"About twelve dollars," she answered. "You know how expensive it is to go that far on the bus."

"That won't buy anything," he groaned. Walking around the store, Rance suddenly shouted, "There's something nice." Strolling over to a display case, he pointed to a huge silver platter.

"Yes," Kelly admitted, "it's beautiful. I just don't think we can afford one hundred and fifty dollars."

"Can I help you folks?" a happy voice broke in.

Looking behind him, Rance recognized the store owner's smiling face. "We're just looking for something for Mom."

"Well, you've come to the right place!" Then, as he noticed the boy's hand, he added, "Nice glove you've got there, Rance. Is it new?"

"Sure is," Rance answered proudly. "It's one of Nolan Ryan's. A real pro model."

"My son loves Nolan," the man answered. "Is that his autograph?" he inquired, pointing to the name written in bold, black ink.

"You bet," Rance boasted.

"Want to sell it?" the man asked.

"You must be kidding!" Rance laughed. Turning, the boy stared at the tray. He looked at his reflection in the polished silver.

"I might trade you the glove for that tray," the owner offered. "It would make a great Mother's Day gift."

"No, I couldn't give up the glove," Rance said.

Pulling him to one side, Kelly whispered, "I thought you said you wanted a really good gift for Mom?"

"Yes, but I can't give up my glove!" Rance said.

"Rance, it's for Mom," Kelly said.

Walking away from his sister, Rance stared at the glove for a long time. Nolan Ryan was his hero. Then it struck him.

"Nolan always gives his best," he sighed to himself. "I should give my best, too." He slowly pulled the glove off and walked over to the store owner. Looking at the tray and then at the glove, he thought about how hard his mother had worked to sell the seeds to earn him the prize. She would really enjoy the tray, and she deserved it.

"I'll tell you what I'll do," Rance said to the owner, a pained expression etched across his face. "I'll trade you the glove for the tray, but I want it engraved."

"Now, I'm not even sure the glove is worth what that tray costs," the owner mused. "I mean, the engraving takes work and. . . ."

"Would twelve dollars cover the engraving?" Kelly asked.

The store owner nodded his head.

"Great!" she exclaimed. "I'll come back later this afternoon to pick it up."

By the time she had turned around, Rance was already out the door. Hurrying, she caught up and the two of them walked in silence all the way home.

The next morning Kelly and Rance woke up early, hurried downstairs, and fixed breakfast. They were just finishing when their mother came into the kitchen, a shocked expression on her face.

"Wake me if I am dreaming," she said, "but I just checked your rooms and they're as neat as two pins. And when did you learn how to cook?"

"Our rooms will stay neat," Kelly assured her. "You have enough to do without us adding to it."

"I hope you like the breakfast," Rance added.

Leaning against the cabinet, Mrs. McGill considered her children's strange behavior and then asked, "Are you in some kind of trouble at school?"

Before they could answer, the doorbell rang.

"I'll get it," Mrs. McGill said. When she opened the door a woman greeted her with a shy smile. A little girl was holding her hand.

"Does a Kelly McGill live here?" the woman asked. "I need to speak to her about something she and my daughter did."

"I knew this morning was too good to be true," Mrs. McGill sighed. "I wonder what she's done now!"

Before she could call them, the two children joined their mother on the front porch. Looking toward the girl, the woman asked, "Kelly?"

"Yes," Kelly answered.

"I'm Rose Watson, Phyllis' mother."

"Oh, I'm glad to meet you," Kelly smiled. "You've got a great little girl."

"Thank you," Mrs. Watson said as she nodded her head. "If she turns out half as well as you have, I'll consider myself a great mother. To go out of your way and spend your own money just to make sure Phyllis got home and then to find someone to take care of her until I got back from my mother's, that was wonderful. I still don't know how the baby sitter and Phyllis got separated. But I have my child back, thanks to you. If she hadn't been there when I got home, I would have been frantic."

"It was nothing," Kelly shrugged.

"I just wanted to tell you and your mother what a great kid you are," the woman said. Looking at Kelly's mother, she added, "You've done a super job."

Kelly smiled and said, "I'm just glad that little Phyllis has a mom who loves her as much as my mom loves me."

After the woman and her daughter left, Kelly and Rance walked with their mother back into the house.

"We have something special for you!" Rance exclaimed. "I'll get it."

When he came back, the three of them sat on the couch, Mrs. McGill in the middle holding a big, flat box. "I wonder what it is?" she smiled.

"Open it," they begged.

As she slowly unwrapped the silver tray, she gasped, "Where did you get the money for something like this?"

"I'll tell you," Kelly volunteered. After Kelly had finished explaining about the baseball glove, Mrs. McGill looked into Rance's face.

"You didn't have to do that," she said.

"I wanted to," he answered. "Besides, this will last longer than a glove. I've still got the good one you bought me last year. And don't forget, Kelly used the money she was saving for new clothes to get it engraved."

Holding the tray up to the light, Mrs. McGill studied the words that her children had placed on her present. Tears filled her eyes as she read, *"To Mom on Mother's Day – You have done too much for us, and we will never be able to do enough for you. We hope that we are worth all your hard work."*

Holding the tray tightly in her arms, Mrs. McGill looked at Kelly and Rance.

"Yes," she sighed. "And you're worth so much more. You have made being a mother the best job in the world."

"Enough of this mushy stuff," Rance protested. "Let's eat breakfast!"

Mrs. McGill couldn't wait for her husband to return from his business trip so that she could tell him about this remarkable weekend. He would be so proud! As it turned out, they would have more than just a weekend to be proud of. Rance and Kelly had discovered a whole new appreciation of how hard it was to be a mother, and they would both do their parts to make every day seem like Mother's Day.

Mother's Day originated in
May 1907 through an idea
conceived by Anna M. Jarvis
of Philadelphia.
She asked her church to set aside
a special day to recognize
all of the mothers in the congregation.
The idea soon spread coast to coast
and in 1914 President Woodrow Wilson
officially recognized
the second Sunday in May
as Mother's Day.